Animal Crackers

Sue Cowling

Illustrated by Diana Catchpole

FAMILY LEARNING

Jungle Sounds

Chatter - chee - chee!
Who's in the tree?

Squaw - squaw - squawk!
Who wants to talk?

Cro - cro - croak!
Who cracks a joke?

Hiss - hiss - hiss!
Whose sound is this?

Chatter – chee – chee!
Monkey, that's me!

Squawk – squawk – squaw!
Hi! I'm a macaw!

Croak – cro – cro!
Frog here – hello!

I'm a big snake
with a tummy ache!

Patterns

Stripes on a ladybug?
Squares on a bee?
Spots on a snail?
Swirls on me?

Spots on a ladybug,
Stripes on a bee,
Swirls on a snail,
And squares on me!

Very Fishy!

Jellyfishy
Soft and squishy,
I can't see your scales!

Starfish too,
No fins for you –
Not even heads or tails!

Puppy

Flappyears
Lappytongue
Gappyteeth

Yappy.

Moppyhair
Floppyears
Hoppylegs

Happy.

Grippyjaws
Nippylegs
Zippypaws

Puppy.

The Great Escape

An egg is like a prison
For a growing chick

And I've got a little beak –
Pick, pick, pick!

I've waited weeks
For my feathers to sprout
And now I'm coming
OUT!

Duck Pond

Paper bag,
Scraps of bread.

Beady eye,
Bobbing head.

Outstretched hand,
Crusts to eat.

Quacking beak,
Paddling feet.

Clever ducks,
Swim, swam, swum.

Gobbled up
Every crumb!

Riddle

None for the goldfish,
    Two for me,
    Four for my cat,
    And six for the bee.

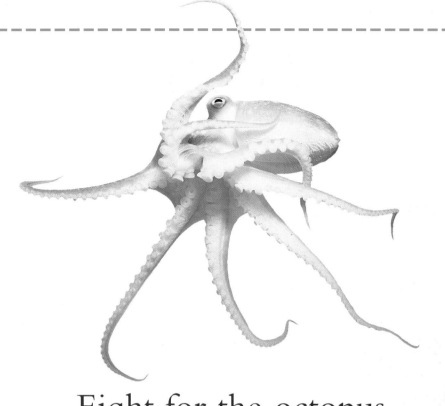

Eight for the octopus
To catch his prey.
Hundreds for the millipede!
What are they?

Anthill

If you find an anthill
And you're ready to dine,
Anteater, anteater,
Read this sign.

If you stick out your tongue,
We'll tickle your snout –
Anteater, anteater,
PLEASE KEEP OUT!

NO EATING!

Crocodile

Just above the water,
Two eyes watching,
Ripples covering
Armored skin.

Just below the water,
Long snout waiting,
Teeth curved
In a great big grin.

Just a little closer,
Closer, closer,
Watching, waiting –
SNAP! You're in!

Rhino Loses His Cool

Someone's been wallowing
In my special pool.
Someone's used my mud pack
To keep himself cool.

Someone's in my dust bath
Enjoying a roll –
One . . . two . . . CHARGE.
This is MY water hole!

Giraffe

Nibble, nibble, nibble!
Munch, swallow, munch!
When his tummy's
having breakfast,
His teeth are
having lunch!